Wild Animal Kingdom

KANGAROOS

NICKI CLAUSEN-GRACE

BLACK
RABBIT
BOOKS

Bolt is published by Black Rabbit Books
P.O. Box 3263, Mankato, Minnesota, 56002.
www.blackrabbitbooks.com
Copyright © 2019 Black Rabbit Books

Jennifer Besel, editor; Catherine Cates, interior
designer; Grant Gould, cover designer;
Omay Ayres, photo researcher

Library of Congress Cataloging-in-Publication Data
Names: Clausen-Grace, Nicki, author.
Title: Kangaroos / by Nicki Clausen-Grace.
Description: Mankato, Minnesota : Black Rabbit Books, [2019] | Series:
Bolt. Wild animal kingdom | Audience: Age 8-12. | Audience: Grade 4 to 6.
|Includes bibliographical references and index.
Identifiers: LCCN 2017029511 (print) | LCCN 2017029933 (ebook) | ISBN
9781680725575 (ebook) | ISBN 9781680724417 (library binding) | ISBN
9781680727357 (paperback)
Subjects: LCSH: Kangaroos—Juvenile literature.
Classification: LCC QL737.M35 (ebook) | LCC QL737.M35 C54 2019
(print) | DDC 599.2/22—dc23
LC record available at https://lccn.loc.gov/2017029511

Printed in China. 3/18

Contents

CHAPTER 1

A Day in the Life

Two male kangaroos face off in a boxing match. They are fighting to **mate** with a female. They bob and weave, throwing punches. Finally, the bigger kangaroo kicks its opponent hard. It wins the fight!

Fascinating Marsupials

Kangaroos are amazing fighters. They are also really interesting animals. There are actually about 65 kangaroo **species**. The most well-known species are the red and gray kangaroos.

All kangaroos are **marsupials**. Their babies cannot survive outside after they're born. Female kangaroos, or does, have pouches for their babies to grow in.

HOW BIG ARE KANGAROOS?

RED KANGAROO

MUSKY RAT KANGAROO

ABOUT 1 FOOT
(.3 m) long

EARS

EYES

KANGAROO FEATURES

TAIL

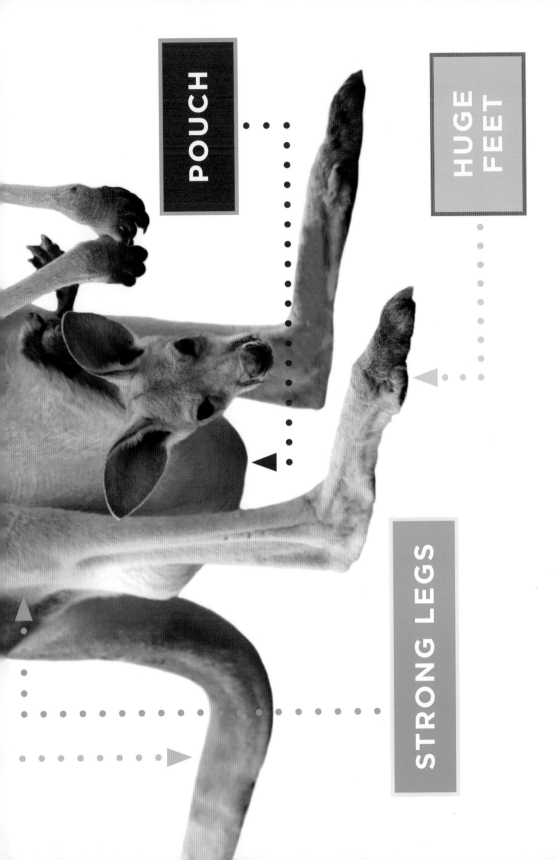

POUCH

HUGE FEET

STRONG LEGS

CHAPTER 2

Food to Eat

and a Place to Live

Most kangaroos live in dry **climates**. They have **adapted** to need very little water. They get most of their water from food.

Almost all kangaroos are herbivores. They eat grass, flowers, and other plants. Some tree kangaroos will eat eggs, birds, and insects too.

Red kangaroos can go two or three months without a drink of water.

Eating Their Greens

Kangaroos have adaptations to help them **digest** plants. Their front teeth are sharp for biting off tough stems. Their back teeth are made for grinding. After swallowing food, they bring it back up. They chew food a second time. This process helps them get all the plants' **nutrients**.

Kangaroos lick their forearms and chests to keep cool. They do this instead of sweating.

The Land Down Under

Kangaroos live in Australia and Papua New Guinea. They live in places that have plants to eat. Some live in forest trees. Others live on the ground in grassy plains or **savannas**.

WHERE KANGAROOS LIVE

Kangaroo Range Map

CHAPTER 3

Family Life

Kangaroos are very social. They live in groups called mobs. Mobs can have more than 100 members. Kangaroos touch noses to connect. They also groom each other. Kangaroos thump their tails on the ground to warn when danger is near.

Living in Mobs

connecting

grooming

warning

COMPARING SIZES

newborn
red kangaroo

1 INCH
(3 centimeters)
.0025 POUND
(1 gram)

**adult female
red kangaroo**

37 INCHES
(94 cm)
88 POUNDS
(39,916 g)

INCHES 0 4

POUNDS 0 10

Newborns

Female kangaroos take care of their young. Females usually give birth to one joey at a time. Newborns are tiny, blind, and hairless. Right after birth, they climb into their mothers' pouches. They nurse and grow in there.

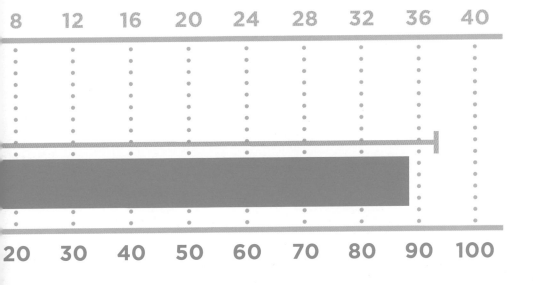

Joeys

Joeys live in their mothers' pouches for up to a year. As they grow, they leave the pouches for short periods. They come back to sleep and eat.

When they are grown, females stay with their mothers' mobs. Males eventually leave to find new groups.

Kangaroos can swim.

Kangaroo Food Chain

This food chain shows what kangaroos eat.
It also shows what eats kangaroos.

EAGLES

DINGOES

FOXES

KANGAROOS

LEAVES   FLOWERS   GRASS

CHAPTER 4

Predators and Other Threats

Kangaroos are mostly shy, peaceful creatures. Even so, they face threats. Eagles and foxes hunt joeys. Dingoes are a type of wild dog. They **prey** on young and adult kangaroos.

Human Threats

Humans are also a threat to kangaroos. People hunt them for their meat and skins. Farmers kill kangaroos to get them out of their crops. People have also moved into kangaroos' habitats. The animals have fewer places to live and less food to eat.

The number of kangaroos is shrinking. People are trying to help these unique animals. But without change, these animals could become extinct.

By the Numbers

2
NUMBER OF JOEYS A MOTHER CAN NURSE AT ONE TIME

30 FEET
(9 m)
DISTANCE A GRAY KANGAROO CAN GO IN ONE HOP

9 to 23 YEARS
LIFE SPAN
in the wild

ABOUT 1

NUMBER OF MONTHS A MOTHER IS PREGNANT

43 MILES
(70 kilometers) per hour

TOP SPEED OF A RED KANGAROO

adapt (uh-DAPT)—to change something so it works better or is better suited for a purpose

climate (KLAHY-mit)—the usual weather conditions in a particular place or region

digest (DY-jest)—to change the food eaten into a form that can be used by the body

marsupial (mar-SOO-pee-uhl)—a kind of mammal that usually has a pouch on the female to carry young

mate (MAYT)—to join together to produce young

nutrient (NYOO-tree-ent)—a substance or ingredient a person or animal needs to be healthy

prey (PRAY)—to catch and eat something

savanna (suh-VAH-nuh)—a grassland containing scattered trees

species (SPEE-seez)—a class of individuals that have common characteristics and share a common name

BOOKS

Franks, Katie. *Kangaroos.* The Zoo's Who's Who. New York: PowerKids Press, 2015.

Meister, Cari. *Do You Really Want to Meet a Kangaroo?* Do You Really Want to Meet… ? Mankato, MN: Amicus Illustrated/Amicus Ink, 2016.

Riggs, Kate. *Kangaroos.* Seedlings. Mankato, MN: Creative Education/Creative Paperbacks, 2017.

WEBSITES

Kangaroo
kids.nationalgeographic.com/animals/ kangaroo/#kangaroo-hopping.jpg

Kangaroo
www.kidsplanet.org/factsheets/kangaroo.html

Kangaroo and Wallaby
animals.sandiegozoo.org/animals/kangaroo- and-wallaby

INDEX